Truth & Tails is Phoebe Kirk, Ben Galley and Alice Reeves. This is what you get when you mix together three like-minded, passionate people who just happen to be an excellent illustrator, a successful self-published author and a professional digital marketer.

Our mission is to use children's fiction to eliminate prejudice, encourage acceptance and aid understanding by addressing hard-to-deal-with concepts - from social issues to scientific theories - through simple, sensitive and beautiful stories featuring loveable characters.

We don't just want to write stories that are educational, we want to become a part of creating a culture of acceptance and understanding in the next generation.

Find out more at www.truthandtails.com

Paperback ISBN: 978-0-9933622-3-1
1st Edition - Published by Truth & Tails LLP
Cover Design by Phoebe Kirk
Written by Truth & Tails LLP

Presents

Vincent the Vixen

Dedicated to everyone who has ever felt like Vincent

Alice

Vincent the Fox loved playing with his brothers and sisters.

Sometimes the fox cubs played hide and seek in the woods.

Sometimes they all went swimming in the stream.

Sometimes they all played tricks
on the farmer's grumpy old cat.
Whatever the fox cubs did together,
they always had lots of fun.

When mum and dad needed peace and quiet, the fox cubs went to Betty the Badger's house to play.

They loved running around the winding tunnels, but the best thing about Betty's house was the dressing up box full of her old clothes.

The fox cubs laughed at
the old-fashioned dresses,
draped themselves in the jewellery
and wobbled around in
the high-heeled shoes.

Vincent loved dressing up more
than anything in the world,
because he could use his imagination
to be anything he wanted to be.

Sometimes he was a rich queen sitting on the throne, watching over her whole kingdom.

Sometimes he was an evil witch making potions out of snails, slugs, bugs and other slimy things.

Sometimes he was a famous performer, delighting crowds of adoring fans.

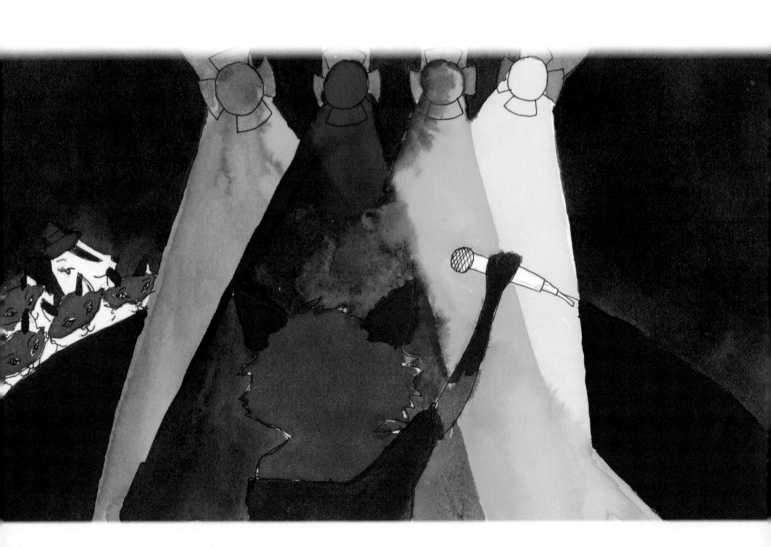

One day, Vincent's brothers
and sisters asked him:
"Vincent, why do you always pretend to
be girls when we play dress up?"

Vincent didn't know what to say. He had never really thought about it before. All of a sudden he didn't feel much like playing.

He took off his dress and shoes and wandered through the tunnels until he found a quiet place to think.

Vincent wondered whether he might be different from his brothers and sisters.

The fox cubs enjoyed doing lots of things together, but his brothers seemed happy being boys and his sisters seemed happy being girls.

Whenever they played dress up, Vincent felt happiest when he wore beautiful dresses.

Whenever they played make-believe, Vincent loved being queens and witches.

Whenever he was just being Vincent, he wished he could be more like his sisters.

When Vincent went to bed that night, he took a long time to fall asleep because he kept thinking about what his brothers and sisters had asked him.

When he finally drifted off to sleep,
he dreamt of the dressing up box
and all the possibilities it held.

The next day, when Vincent was on his way home from school, he spotted Betty the Badger picking fruit for her dinner.

"Hello Vincent," said Betty. "You seemed quite sad yesterday, which isn't like you at all. What was the matter?"

"Oh, it's nothing," replied Vincent. He didn't think he could explain the way he was feeling.

"Was it something your brothers and sisters said that made you sad?" asked Betty, "You all play together so happily when you visit my house!"

"Yes," said Vincent. "They asked why I always want to be girl characters when we play dress up."

Betty smiled. "Why does that matter, Vincent?" she asked.

Vincent took a deep breath and said: "It's because I think I'm really a girl."

Betty nodded. "In that case, I have a story that might help you," she said.

When I was a young badger I loved playing make-believe with my sisters, just like you. When I was a young badger I was also a boy, just like you.

I started to think that maybe I was really a girl badger. I couldn't stop thinking that way, so I told my sisters how I was feeling.

At first they were confused because they didn't feel the same way, but they all listened patiently while I explained.

From that day on, I've been Betty the Badger and I've been happy ever since.

After hearing Betty's story, Vincent felt a lot less sad. "Thank you, Betty," he said. He smiled all the way home. He was still smiling at dinner time.

"You seem very happy today, Vincent!" said his mum.

"I am," replied Vincent. "It's because I know who I am now."

"What wonderful news!" exclaimed his dad, "but what do you mean?"

"Everyone knows I love dressing up and playing make-believe," said Vincent, "but I'm really a girl fox even when I'm not playing make-believe."

At first Vincent's family were puzzled
but the more they listened to
Vincent talk about his feelings,
the more they understood.

From that day on, instead of being a boy fox, Vincent grew up and she lived happily as Vincent the Vixen.

Acknowledgements

A very special thank you goes to Matt Horwood from Stonewall as well as Elly, Aimee and Maeve for their constructive feedback, welcome critique and kind words.

It's important to note that Vincent's experience is just one fox's story of the exploration and expression of their gender identity.

For more information, www.stonewall.org.uk is a great place to start.

Lightning Source UK Ltd.
Milton Keynes UK
UKIC03n1947060316
269643UK00015B/74